A Gift For:

_____

From:

_____

Snow What Fun!
When Snowmen Come to Life on Christmas Eve
Copyright © 2004 Hallmark Licensing, LLC

The Snowbelly Family of Chillyville Inn
Copyright © 2005 Hallmark Licensing, LLC

The Snow Must Go On!
A Way, Way Off-Broadway Adventure
Copyright © 2006 Hallmark Licensing, LLC

Snow Happy to be Here!
The Slightly Silly Story of the Snowblatt Family
Copyright © 2007 Hallmark Licensing, LLC

Snow Place Like Home!
The Incredible Snowkids of Marshmallow Mountain
Copyright © 2008 Hallmark Licensing, LLC

Snow Wonder We're Friends!
Copyright © 2009 Hallmark Licensing, LLC

The Snowman Band of Snowboggle Bend
Copyright © 2010 Hallmark Licensing, LLC

What's Shakin' in Snowflake City?
Copyright © 2011 Hallmark Licensing, LLC

There's Snow Stopping Us Now!
Copyright © 2012 Hallmark Licensing, LLC

Snow Time to Lose
The Shiverdale Snowbuddies Save the Day
Copyright © 2013 Hallmark Licensing, LLC

There's Snowbody Like You!
Copyright © 2014 Hallmark Licensing, LLC

There's Snow Time Like Cookie Time!
Copyright © 2015 Hallmark Licensing, LLC

Magical Sleigh? Snow Way!
Copyright © 2016 Hallmark Licensing, LLC

Rex Snows the Way to Grandma's
Copyright © 2017 Hallmark Licensing, LLC

Snow Letter Left Behind
Copyright © 2018 Hallmark Licensing, LLC

Contents

3

Snow What fun!

when snowmen come to life on Christmas eve

A STORY FROM THE HALLMARK HOLIDAY SERIES

Written by Cheryl Hawkinson and Illustrated by Mike Esberg

'Twas the night before Christmas, and all through the land,
the snowfolks were stirring according to plan.

They sprang into life in a fluffy white flurry
and fled from their yards in a great big fat hurry,
into the streets, where they shouted with glee,
"Hooray, now it's time for the Snow Jubilee!"

They clumped and they clustered, said "Howdy and Hi,"
then smooshed into snow clouds and swooshed through the sky,
past forests and rivers and over a knoll
to a most secret place that's just south of North Pole.

From all over the planet, they started arriving
and greeting each other with hugs and high-fiving.
'Twas their once-a-year snow night, their big rendezvous,
but first they had something important to do.

"Look," someone shouted. "Up there—it's his sleigh!
We've got to guide Santa—no time to delay!"

So quickly they lined up (their form was perfection)
and waved Santa's sleigh in a southbound direction.

Then they took their banjos, their flutes, and their drums.

They sang silly songs, and they hummed happy hums.

They waltzed and they polka'd. They jived and they jumped.

They pranced and they chicken-danced. Man, were they pumped!

They staged a big contest with fabulous games.
They awarded the winners and called out their names . . .

9

Now Slushy,

now Freezy,

now Twirly,

now Twiggles.

On Jingle,

on Bingle,

on Wheezy,

on Wiggles.

They snapped on their snowshoes,
their skis, and their skates
and barreled about at incredible rates.

And when they were tired, they flopped to the ground,
enjoying their bird friends who flocked all around,
feeding them seeds they had brought in big sacks.
(It felt really good just to rest and relax.)

Then suddenly they could hear bells in the air.
"It's Santa—he's back and he's got gifts to spare!"
The snowfolks looked upward and grinned at the sight
of packages raining down into the night.

"Wow, what a fabulous Snow Jubilee—
but the night's almost over, so we'd better flee!
We've helped out old Santa and had some fun, too.
Mission accomplished—it's time to skiddoo!"

Softly they swooped up in balls of white fluff
and lumpily, bumpily flew fast enough
to arrive in their places before the sun rose
and return (every one!) to their regular pose.

Now maybe you're thinking it's hard to believe
that snowpeople come to life each Christmas Eve.
But look out your window first thing Christmas Day . . .
and see if your snowman looks quite the same way!

The Snowbelly Family
of Chillyville Inn

A STORY FROM THE HALLMARK HOLIDAY SERIES

Written by Cheryl Hawkinson and Illustrated by Mike Esberg

It's holiday time at the Chillyville Inn,
and the Snowbelly family is in quite a spin.
There's so much to do—who can rest?

Grandpa is greeting the folks at the door,
in addition to handling his favorite chore—
carving a gift for each guest.

Inside the inn, there are songs in the air,
as Papa plays piano with fabulous flair . . .
with a solo from Twiggles the dog.

Mama is bustling around with a tray
of slippery ice slushies and ice-cream soufflé
plus a pitcher of icy cold nog.

16

And the tree! What a tree! How the icicles glitter!
And look, you can see there's a mighty fine knitter
who lives here and Grandma's her name!

As Snowbert and Snowbelle are topping the tree,
Grandma keeps knitting—and quite rapidly—
until she is heard to exclaim . . .

"Land sakes, I forgot—I've got yarn outside soaking.
Kids, won't you please take some sticks and start poking
to check on my red and green dye?"

So Snowbelle and Snowbert go out by the barn
and start stirring and swirling the two vats of yarn—
and holding up strands to the sky.

When who should appear as if out of the blue?
Jingles the mischievous kitten—that's who.
(Last seen, she was napping in bed.)

Miss Jingles jumps up with spectacular speed,
gets tangled in yarn like a cat tumbleweed,
and when she rolls out, she's bright red!

Well, Twiggles the dog simply can't be outdone.

He figures that *he* is the Master of Fun

and wants to be part of the scene.

So he lurches and lunges at Jingles the cat,

tips over a vat with a very big splat—

and now he is totally green!

When Snowbert and Snowbelle catch up with their pets,

they hold them and scold them, expressing regrets,

all gathered around in a huddle.

Then they look at each other and whisper, "No way!

What will we do? What will Ma and Pa say?

We look like a red and green muddle!"

They troop back inside, and all four fear the worst . . .

. . . but when Ma and Pa see them, they can't help but burst
into laughter and blurt out with glee,

"You look just like Christmas! Well, what do you know!
These things tend to happen when you're made of snow.
We need pictures! Most definitely!"

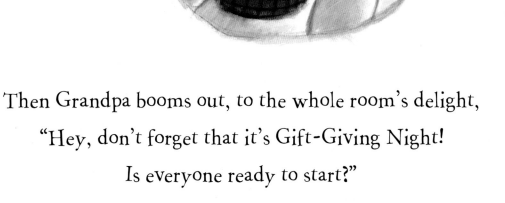

Then Grandpa booms out, to the whole room's delight,
"Hey, don't forget that it's Gift-Giving Night!
Is everyone ready to start?"

21

A mad scramble ensues, and more fun is unloosed
as presents, once hidden, are quickly produced.
Oh, here comes the really good part . . .

Everyone's thrilled with the gifts they receive,
especially the Snowbelly kids, who believe
that *this* is their best Christmas ever.

On his icicle bicycle, Snowbert goes riding—
he's popping those wheelies! He's hopping! He's sliding!
Does he plan on stopping! No, never!

And Snowbelle can do what she's wished for so long—
with her fresh frozen flute, she performs a sweet song
and melts every heart in the place.

There's a hush in the room, then a voice from the hall
says, "Let's raise a glass to the best inn of all!"
And a smile spreads across every face.

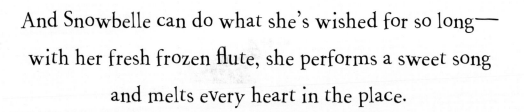

"To the Snowbelly family, for all their good cheer,
and to Chillyville Inn, where we're welcome each year!
A toast to our wonderful hosts!"

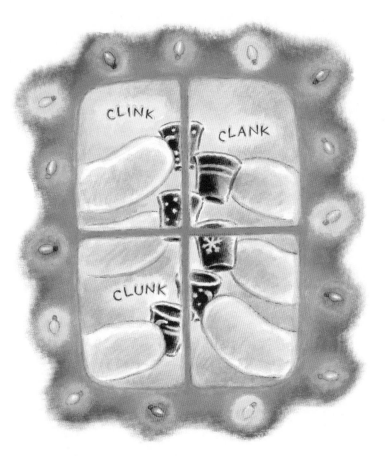

Then as night starts to fall like a big snowy feather,
they all share a hug 'cause they're happy together . . .
And *that* is what matters most.

The Snow Must Go On!

a way, way off-broadway adventure

A STORY FROM THE HALLMARK HOLIDAY SERIES

Written by Molly Wigand and Illustrated by Mike Esberg

The sun shone bright and friendly in the South Pole sky.
On the gleaming glacier below, the snowpeople and penguins of
Antarctic Springs prepared busily for Christmas.
Shoppers hunted for perfect surprises, children made big wishes,
and workers sculpted and decorated the town's shimmering ice tree.
December feels cool and crisp at the bottom of the world,
but warmth and goodwill bustled in the tiny snow-covered town.

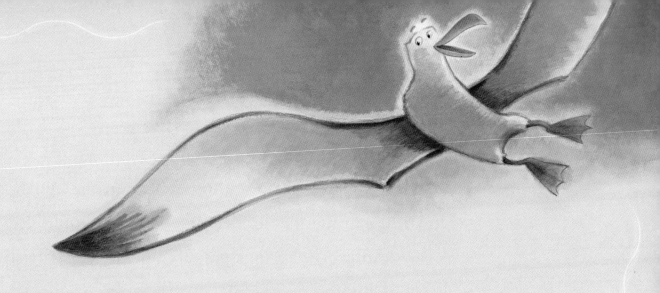

At midday, a silver speck appeared in the eastern sky.
It grew larger and larger until all eyes were on the brilliant shape.
"It's the albatross!" yelled a snowman.
The majestic bird flapped over the town square,
casting dusky shadows amidst the sparkle of the snow.
"Come one, come all!" squawked the albatross.
"Mayor Flakely has called a town meeting.
It's urgent! Meet in the square at moonrise!
Come one, come all!"

That evening, as the moon ascended in the violet sky,
every snowman and snowwoman, every snowkid,
every snowdog and snowcat, and every penguin
great and small hurried to the square.
"Welcome, good citizens!" said Mayor Flakely, a tall,
distinguished snowman with a kind
but booming voice. "Here it is, December again.
Children everywhere are thinking about
one magical wintry wonderland . . .
the marvelous place where happy holidays begin."
"You mean the North Pole?" asked a tiny penguin.
The mayor nodded, a little sadly.
"Yes. The North Pole," he sighed. "But don't you wish
people knew that South Pole folks are merry?
And jolly? And fun?"

27

"The world should hear our story," said Mayor Flakely.

"But how?" everyone asked, in perfect unison.

"We need some big ideas!" said the mayor.

The albatross raised his wing. "How about a cool slogan?

Like, um, 'Antarctica. Cold, and lots of it.'"

"Some slogan," muttered a penguin.

"Maybe we could offer a fancy cruise," suggested a snowmom.

Mayor Flakely scratched his head. "Hmm . . .

cruises and icebergs? I'm afraid that's not a good fit."

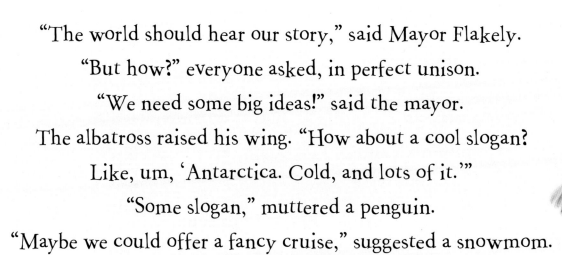

A group of penguins jumped up and down excitedly.

"We know!" they giggled. "Pick us! Pick us!"

"What is it, little friends?" asked the mayor.

"Let's put on a show!" they yelled.

And just like that, it was settled. Antarctic Springs

would put on the biggest, best holiday show ever.

Each penguin and snowperson had a special talent to contribute. One snowman sang a rock-and-roll song: "You ain't nothin' but a reindeer, flyin' all the time. You ain't nothin' but a reindeer, flyin' all the time. You ain't never seen a penguin, and you ain't no friend of mine!"

Another snowman practiced a magic trick. "Watch me pull a penguin out of my hat! Nothing up my sleeve! Presto!"
The penguin squirmed in the snowman's mitten. "Ouch!" yelled the penguin. "Watch the feathers, buster!"

Strains of "The Nutcracker Suite" filled the air over the town's skating rink. Three young girl penguins leaped and twirled to the music.
"Point your flippers," said the snowwoman teacher.
"Looks pretty now. Listen! It's 'Waltz of the Flowers!' Be a flower!"
"What's a flower?" asked one of the penguins.

Another penguin brought a big kettle to the town square. "I will now juggle fifteen fish with my foot flippers," he boasted. One at a time, he added fish to his juggling show. "And . . . behind the back!" he continued. "Blindfolded! Ta-dah!"

A big, burly comedian used a stick for a microphone. "So a snowman walks into an ice-cream shop. The clerk says, 'Go away. We're closed.' Snowman says, 'C'mon. Let me in! I'm an ice guy!' Get it? An! Ice! Guy! A nice guy! Is this thing on?" the comedian joked, tapping the microphone stick with his hand. "Whoa. Chilly room."

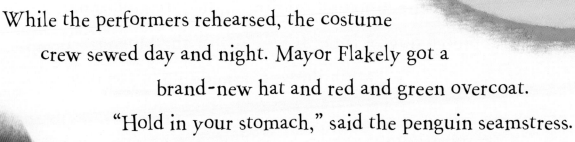

While the performers rehearsed, the costume crew sewed day and night. Mayor Flakely got a brand-new hat and red and green overcoat. "Hold in your stomach," said the penguin seamstress. "I am holding it in," chuckled the mayor.

Soon the songs were all in tune, and the dancers were in step. Workers put finishing touches on a magnificent theater in the glacier valley. The mayor gathered the cast and crew for a meeting. "You know what's wonderful about this show?" he asked. "Every person in town has an important part in its success! Let's hear it for us! Hip-Hip, Hooray!"

As the cheer echoed through the town, a tiny snowgirl raised her hand. "If everyone's in the show," she asked, "who's going to watch it?" Stillness blanketed the crowd.

"Shhh! Did you hear that jingle-jingle?" asked a penguin.
"And the prancing and pawing?" added a snowdog.
Ho! Ho! Ho!

The cast peeked through the curtain. Right there, in the very front row, all the way from the North Pole, was Santa Claus himself and all his reindeer. The snowpeople and penguins performed their hearts out. The show was a smash! "Bravo, South Pole!" yelled Santa, jumping to his feet. "You've proven that North, South, East, or West, it's the joy inside our hearts that counts at Christmas!" And at that magical moment, in that tiny Antarctic town, everyone felt merry . . . and jolly . . . and absolutely on top of the world.

Snow Happy to be Here!

the Slightly Silly Story of the Snowblatt family

ESBERG

A STORY FROM THE HALLMARK HOLIDAY SERIES

Written by Cheryl Hawkinson and Illustrated by Mike Esberg

One day the Snowblatts were having a chat,
as they do when the humans aren't near,
when suddenly little Snow-Ellen piped up
and said in a voice crystal clear—

"Where do we come from, and why were we made,
and how did we get here from there?"
"Yeah," joined in Snow-John, "I want to know, too.
Did we—POOF!—just appear from thin air?"

Papa

Snow-Ellen

Mama

Snow-John

Mama and Papa just winked at each other.
"Good question!" said Mama. "Let's see,
maybe it's time that I tell you the tale
of how snowpeople all come to be.

"It starts with the snowflakes that fly from the sky
to wherever on earth they are blown—
zillions of snowflakes, but each one unique
with a destiny all of its own.

"Some will be snowballs, and some will be forts,
and some will melt down to the sea.
Some will be skied on, and some will be slid on,
and some will become you and me!"

"But how do these snowflakes get made into us?"
said the snowkids with some consternation.
"I'll answer that," replied Papa Snowblatt—
"It's location, location, LOCATION!"

"What Papa is saying," continued his wife,
"is that snowflakes are only the start.
There have to be fun-loving humans nearby,
because they do the magical part.

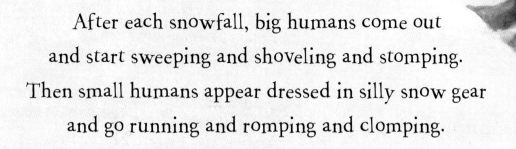

After each snowfall, big humans come out
and start sweeping and shoveling and stomping.
Then small humans appear dressed in silly snow gear
and go running and romping and clomping.

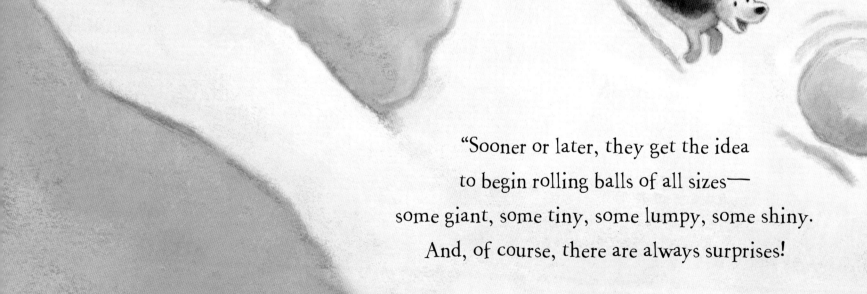

"Sooner or later, they get the idea
to begin rolling balls of all sizes—
some giant, some tiny, some lumpy, some shiny.
And, of course, there are always surprises!

"When they start attacking the issue of stacking,
they find that it's not very easy.
There's huffing and puffing and wobbling and bobbling
that leave the poor things kind of wheezy.

"Then comes the part where we get all our features—
our eyes, ears, and noses, and such.
As you may have noticed, materials vary,
so we each get that personal touch."

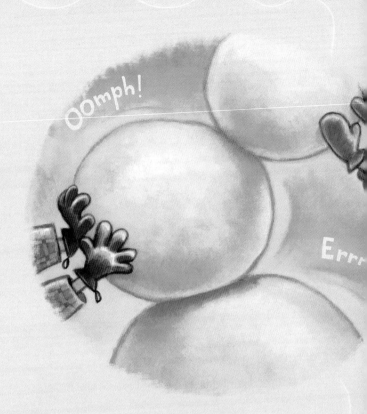

Oomph!

Errr

Stinky

Ms. Natural

Capt. Icebuckle

Trooper

Sugar

Slick

Fifi

Tooley

"Yeah, that's for sure," Snow-John said with a grin.
"You know we all look kind of weird.
Plus, none of us match each other at all,
and just think about Grandpa's beard!"

"That's right," said Snow-Ellen, "and how about clothes?
Have you ever seen such funny stuff?
Hey, wait there a minute," said Papa Snowblatt,
you're focusing on the mere fluff."

"I agree," added Mama. "You're missing the point.
It's a miracle we're even here.
Our humans may not have the best taste in fashion,
but they know what they're doing, that's clear.

"After they've rolled us and buttoned and bowed us
and patted down each little flake,
they step back with pride, and then they provide
what we need to be finally awake."

"What is it? What is it?" exclaimed the snowkids.
"Is it hard? Does it take a long while?"
"No," explained Mama, "it just takes a moment—
they bring us to life when they smile."

Snow place like Home!

the Incredible Snow kids of marshmallow mountain

ESBERG

A STORY FROM THE HALLMARK HOLIDAY SERIES

Written by Diana Manning and Illustrated by Mike Esberg

The snowkids of Marshmallow Mountain were meeting
one troublesome Tuesday at two.
They all gathered round in their clubhouse,
Fort Snowpack, to try to decide what to do.

Then Snow-Joe (their president) rose to his feet.
"My dad says this place used to rock!
There were tourists and festivals all through the year,
and stuff going on round the clock!

MARSHMALLOW MOUNTAIN'S
25th ANNUAL
CANDY EXTRAVAGANZA!
featuring
THE WORLD'S MOST MARVELOUS,
MOUTH-WATERING SWEETS!
DECIDEDLY DELICIOUS DELICACIES!
TRULY TASTY TREATS!

"'Cause Marshmallow Mountain was known as the home
of the world's most incredible candy . . ."
"So THAT'S what they made in that empty old factory
on Candy Cane Lane!" added Andy.

"Hey, let's check it out!" said the twins, Fridge and Midge,
and all of the snowkids agreed.
They started out walking . . . all except Spike,
who snowboarded there at top speed!

47

Snow-Joe explained as they wandered inside,
"That's the Candy Contraption, you know!
The famous machine that made all kinds of treats . . .
but I guess it broke down years ago."

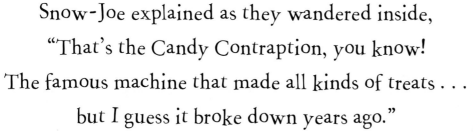

"I bet I could find some spare parts for that thing,"
said Spike, whose ideas were great.
He knew all the junkyards that had the best stuff
for the sculptures he liked to create.

"And I'll find the recipes!" Freeze Louise offered.
"I bet they've been all tucked away
in grandmothers' cookbooks and family kitchens.
I better start looking today!"

Fridge and Midge painted some colorful flyers
their fine feathered friends could deliver.
Snow-Joe and Andy sped off on their skates
to tell all the snowfolk downriver.
Soon everyone heard what the snowkids were doing.
"I tell you, those kids have got spunk!"
"There hasn't been this much excitement in town
since the Candy Contraption went CLUNK!"

Then Snow-Joe announced it was time for a test.
Each pulley and gear was in place,
each special ingredient poured in the hopper,
a huge, hopeful smile on each face.

The wheels started whirring! The spoons started stirring!
And out popped one peppermint kiss.
They waited . . . and waited . . . 'til Freeze Louise shouted,
"It's GOT to go faster than THIS!"

Then Andy's quick brain made some quick calculations
and soon he'd adjusted each dial.
Then candy came rocketing out by the dozens,
creating a mountainous pile!

The snowkids got busy with boxing and bagging
(and tasting a sample or two).
They labeled and loaded and made their deliveries,
and each had a fun job to do!

51

The news got around that the snowkids had done it!
They'd gotten things rolling again!
And Marshmallow Mountain was just as exciting
as snowfolk remembered "back when."

From Shiverdale Corners to Snowberry Falls,

Chill Valley to Icicle Run,

they came for a taste of that world-famous candy . . .

and stayed for the warm, friendly fun.

Snow Wonder We're friends!

A STORY FROM THE HALLMARK HOLIDAY SERIES

Written by Molly Wigand and Illustrated by Mike Esberg

The week before Christmas,
Brianna and Brendan were bouncing right off of the walls.
From morning 'til night, the kids giggled and played
while their mom worked at decking the halls!

Mom needed a break, so she sent the kids out
(with a warm, woolly hat on each noggin).
They tromped through the snow to an old backyard shed
and pulled out the family toboggan.

Determined to have an exciting adventure,
they headed for Daredevil Hill.
They'd heard there was magic and mystery there—
and they DID love a wild winter thrill!

As the kids looked straight down from the hill's scary summit,

the feathery snow sparkled and swirled.

This was no bunny slope— but they were both ready

to sled into that magical world!

"This is awesome!" cried Brendan. "Hot dog!" yelled Brianna.

"Look out below, everyone!"

Then they took a deep breath and zoomed down the hill.

"Wheeeeee!" Brendan squealed. "This is fun!"

The children went faster and faster and FASTER!
Past snow-covered pine trees they sped!
At this dizzying pace, they could hardly see straight—
no one saw the big bump up ahead.

The toboggan went BAM!
then flew up in the air but didn't crash back in the snow.
It kept soaring upward—much higher and quicker
than normal toboggans should go!

Over rooftops and treetops at super warp speed,
the wind tossed the toboggan around.
It swayed side to side,
then did twelve loop-de-loops . . .

. . . before landing KER-PLUNK! on the ground.

They brushed themselves off and began to explore
this look-alike town they were in.
"Check it out!" Brendan said. "That snowgirl looks like you,
and her snowbrother could be my twin!"

The snowkids were running and jumping and playing
and driving Snow Mom up the wall!
So she sent them outside (like Brianna and Brendan)
in their boots, hats, mittens, and all!

From the moment they met, those four kids had a blast.
(In spite of the blustery weather!)
After snow forts and snow pies, the friends all decided
to make a new snowpal together!

They rolled up some snowballs and packed them and stacked them
'til—*voila!* They'd built a snowguy!
And as soon as they gave him stick arms and a mouth,
the coolest jokes started to fly!

There were knock-knocks and limericks and silly snow songs!
"Deck the halls with baloney!" he said.
"Jingle bells! Santa smells!"
Cracking jokes, making faces—
this comic was knocking 'em dead!

"Have an ice day!"
"Snow wonder we're friends!" No line was too silly or punny!
"Do you think it will rain, deer?" he joked with a chuckle—
there just was no end to the funny!

Soon it was time for the kids to go home.
No one wanted this great day to end!
But Brianna and Brendan got ready to leave
(along with their little snowfriend)!

They said their good-byes, and with hugs all around,
they wrapped up the little guy tight.
The snowkids helped out with a one, two, three . . . push!
And the toboggan sailed off out of sight!

In less than an instant,
Brianna and Brendan were home with a story to share . . .
of a magical land filled with frosty good fun
and the snowfolks who'd welcomed them there!

And still to this day (after many long winters)
the snowguy, so funny and small,
reminds the whole family that laughter and friends
are the very best presents of all!

The Snowman Band
of
Snowboggle Bend

A STORY FROM THE HALLMARK HOLIDAY SERIES

Written by Cheryl Hawkinson and Illustrated by Mike Esberg

In the far northern village of Snowboggle Bend,
it snowed . . . and it snowed . . .and it snowed without end.

Snow floated and fluttered and silenced the land,
except for the sound of the town's only band.

From a broken-down school bus
their music came soaring,
awakening animals
who'd rather be snoring.

They called themselves Snow Pack,
these talented four,
and they practiced and practiced
and practiced some more.

Snow-Joe blew sweetly
on his alto sax,
while Snow-Freddy's fingers
flew over his axe.

Snow-Tom on trumpet
could make a horn sing,
and Snow-Ken on keys
was a beautiful thing.

There was just one small problem.
No one knew they existed.
It was hard to get gigs,
but Snow Pack persisted.

Each year they made tracks
to a nearby big city
to audition for Slush Fest.
The results were not pretty.

Each year they received
a "Sorry, but no!"
from the concert's promoter,
Sir Farley Fitz-Snow.

"We've got to do something,"
said Snow-Ken at last.
"Let's just GO to the Slush Fest.
It might be a blast!"

"But how do we get there?"
said Snow-Joe with a frown.
"The Snow Dome Pavilion
is way out of town."

"Well, our bus is no help,"
sadly answered Snow-Freddy,
"Its get-up is gone
and it's hardly road-ready."

"There's someone," said Snow-Tom,
"who might fix it for us.
She's quite the mechanic,
my sister Snow-Doris."

"I'll fix it," Sis said,
soon after arriving.
"But when I'm all finished,
then *I'll* do the driving."

"But where are the mammoths?"
demanded Snow-Joe.
"Our town's team of woolies
should shovel this snow!"

Sure enough, the two mammoths
showed up at the scene,
but they wouldn't budge—
they were moody and mean.

So Snow Pack left town
with some rattling and creaking,
but at the first curve
they heard shouting and shrieking.

A huge crowd had gathered
by the Mountain Pass Ranch.
The band cried out loudly,
"Oh, no! Avalanche!"

"No one can move!
Everyone's stuck!
Goodbye, good old Slush Fest.
Man, what bad luck!"

"Hey," said Snow Freddy,
"No one's leaving here soon.
We've got an audience—
let's play 'em some tunes."

So they turned up their amps
and they really got swinging.
And soon EVERYBODY
was clapping and singing.

Then someone said "Look,
the mammoths are movin'!
Who knew they liked music?
They really are groovin!"

Sure enough, the two woolies
were smiling and dancing.
You would think they were reindeer,
the way they were prancing.

Then quick as a flash
the two creatures had cleared
a path through the mountains
and everyone cheered!

When who should appear
but Sir Farley Fitz-Snow,
saying, "Good job, you guys.
What a band! What a show!

"This is kind of last minute,
but what do you say?
Could you be the star act
at the Slush Fest today?"

72

They all looked at each other,
then replied with a grin,
"Well, we *are* kind of busy,
but we'll fit you in."

What's Shakin' in Snowflake City?

A STORY FROM THE HALLMARK HOLIDAY SERIES

Written by Cheryl Hawkinson and Illustrated by Mike Esberg

All kinds of places
have all kinds of weather,
but the weather in Snowflake
is strange altogether.

In the city of Snowflake
it doesn't just snow,
the ground shakes and rattles
while winds whip and blow.

And it happens so fast
that these storms barely last.
They whoosh in and whoosh out,
and in moments they're past.

Now, the Snowfarkle family
just waits out the shaking.
They don't even mind
when the snowflakes start flaking.

But at holiday time
there's so much to get ready,
it sure isn't helpful
when things are unsteady.

Like that night Papa Snowfarkle
climbed up a tree
and the world started wobbling,
and—oops!—so did he.

Or that day Mama Snowfarkle
stood in her kitchen
and the flour started flying
and the table was twitchin'.

Or that time when the kids
were out skating quite slickly,
and the ice shook and shivered
and cartwheeled them quickly!

Now, all the snow-grown-ups—
they don't bat an eye.
The storms come and go,
and they don't wonder why.

But some of the snowkids
will sometimes discuss,
"How come so much snow
seems to snow down on us?"

"Are there clouds in the sky
who like clomping and stomping?

And when they start dancing
we all take a whomping?"

"Or way far away
are there mountains that grumble?

And when they get angry,
they make this place rumble?"

"Or deep underground
could there be a huge bear
who snores in his sleep
and his roars shake the air?"

Then Mama will laugh
and say "Hey, that's enough!
Where in the world
do you kids get this stuff?"

And Papa will pipe up,
"Your mother is right.
Now scurry inside—
Santa's coming tonight!

If our house shakes a bit,
and the snow swirls around,
as long as we're happy,
let those flakes tumble down!"

So the Snowfarkles gather
for games, songs, and food,
and nothing can bother
their holiday mood.

Then at last they tuck in
to dream their sweet dreams,
not knowing their city's
not quite what it seems . . .

SNOWFLAKE CITY

There's Snow Stopping Us Now!

A STORY FROM THE HALLMARK HOLIDAY SERIES

Written by Cheryl Hawkinson and Illustrated by Mike Esberg

'Twas the day of the annual Mount Icy Run
and the whole town of Snowbelt was ready for fun.
Snowfolks had gathered from far and from near
for the iciest race in the north hemisphere.

Then all of a sudden, from up in the sky,
a big box came falling. What was it, and why?

When all of the snowfolks crept closer to look,
a voice squeaked out "Help!" and the box rocked and shook.

And out popped a penguin with a mischievous smile,
who flashed them a note in a confident style:

The people of Snowbelt were totally stunned.
"Why did you come here? Where are you from?"

"Are you planning to race? But your skis are so tall!
Are you sure that they'll work? You're so small, after all!"

Perry replied, "I'm from the South Pole,
and racing Mount Icy's my big lifetime goal.
The skis are my grandpa's. They're sweet and they're fast.
They're made out of candy, but they're sure built to last."

"Kid, you've got spunk," said a snowkid named Squee.
"I'll help you get started—just stick close to me."
Then Perry and Squee, and his friends Slick and Space,
followed the crowds to the site of the race.

They jumped on the ski lift to ride up Mount Icy.
"Hang on, little Perry," said Squee. "This gets dicey."
They rose higher and higher. The wind snapped and twirled.
"Here we go!" cried out Perry, "to the top of the world!"

But once they got up there and Perry looked down,
he started to shiver and quiver and frown.
He thought to himself, "How can steep be so deep?
I don't think I'm ready to make such a leap."

But he just went along with the rest of the throng.
Then the starting bell rang—and something was wrong!
"Oh no!" shouted Squee. "My Snowfloogle's broken!
My steering is shot and my frack-stack is smokin'!"

Then Perry piped up, "Use my candy cane skis!
I don't mind not racing. Just go ahead, please!"
"Really?" said Squee. "That would be super great.
I'll do you proud, Perry. Just wait at the gate."

Squee put on his skis and tore off down the slope,
with his mind set on winning and his heart full of hope.
But when Perry peered over, he saw that poor Squee
had tangled and mangled his skis in a tree!

Forgetting his fear, Perry took off to help,
sliding down on his belly with a very loud yelp!
He swooped and he swerved with incredible speed,
landing right at the spot where poor Squee had been treed.

Once Perry freed Squee and they shook off some snow,
they looked at each other and said, "Hey, let's go!"

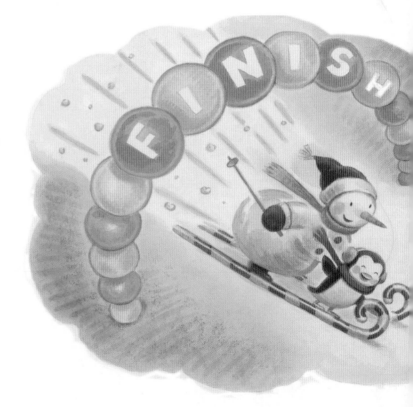

They raced down together, Perry and Squee,
flying fast past the finish with a *whoop* and a *whee*.

"We did it!" said Perry. "My friend and I here!
My big dream came true and I conquered my fear!"
"You did it!" said Squee. "What a guy! What a friend!
That sure was fun, Perry. Let's do it again!"

Snow Time to Lose

The Shiverdale Snowbuddies Save the Day

A STORY FROM THE HALLMARK HOLIDAY SERIES

By Diana Manning and Illustrated by Mike Esberg

In the village of Shiverdale, Finny O'Flurry
is somebody everyone knows—
he's a likable snowguy whose little dog Rex
is with him wherever he goes.

Now, Rex has a habit of getting in trouble.
He really does WANT to be good,
though sometimes the way that he tries to help out
just doesn't turn out like it should.

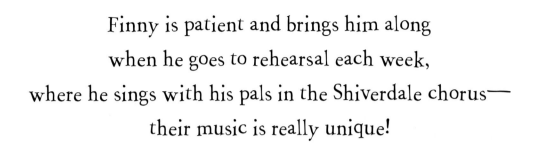

Finny is patient and brings him along
when he goes to rehearsal each week,
where he sings with his pals in the Shiverdale chorus—
their music is really unique!

The chorus is known for their Christmas Eve Sing-Along,
held every year on the square—
snowkids and snow families join in the singing,
and everyone wants to be there!

"It's a Christmas tradition for folks far and near,"
their director says, proud as can be.
"It's a very big deal, so let's be at our best—
we've got to make sure we're on key!"

When practice begins, Finny sings from the heart . . .
while his little dog Rex really HOWLS.
Stopping the music, the stern Mr. Trebleclef
grumpily grumbles and scowls.

"That dog has to go!" he finally declares,
and throws his baton in the street.
But Rex thinks they're playing a fun game of fetch,
and carries it back in his teeth.

Patting his head, Finny sends him on home,
with the promise of treats later on—
Mr. Trebleclef sighs as he turns to his chorus
and takes up his icy baton.

"We've got to be ready! Our honored guest soloists—
both will be joining us soon!
Snowphie Soprano and Baron von Yodel
arriving by hot air balloon!"

Their journey turns out to be freezy and breezy—
poor Snowphie holds on to her hat.
Von Yodel looks over their flight plan again
so he can make sure where they're at.

They land on the roof of Trebleclef's house
where they'll stay as his holiday guests.
"We're honored to have you!" They're greeted with smiles.
"Won't you come in and just rest?"

The very next day when it's time for the Sing-Along,
Trebleclef's nowhere around.
Finny and Rex go to knock on his door
and find icicles down to the ground!

Poor Mr. Trebleclef's trapped in his house
along with the soloists, too—
"Our hot air balloon must have melted the snow!
Now what are we going to do?"

"We've got to get out," Mr. Trebleclef shouts.
"We can't disappoint all our fans!"
Soon everyone hears of their icy dilemma
and comes to help out with a plan.

They try to break through, but the ice is too thick,
and they wonder what they should do next—
when Finny O'Flurry declares, "Not to worry!"
and calls for his little dog Rex.

Popping his head from a snowbank nearby,
the lovable Rex reappears—
"Not HIM again," Trebleclef loudly protests.
"That dog has been trouble for YEARS!"

Then Finny starts singing, with Rex joining in
with an earsplitting howl of a sound—
It rattles the ground, and they hear a big CRACK!
as the icicles all tumble down!

"There's no time to lose!" Mr. Trebleclef shouts,
  "The Sing-Along's ready to start!"
So he and the soloists rush to the square,
  while already singing their parts.

The Shiverdale Sing-Along happens as planned,
  and everyone's really relieved—
the crowd gives a cheer and surrounds Rex and Finny
  as heroes who saved Christmas Eve!

There's Snowbody Like You!

A STORY FROM THE HALLMARK HOLIDAY SERIES

Written by Barbara Loots and Illustrated by Mike Esberg

Chillbert was little as snowchildren go.

He'd been waiting and waiting for his turn to grow.

His dad said, "Don't worry. In no time, you'll be

the star of the team! Just be patient. You'll see!"

Out at the Ice Park, the Whoop-De-Do Slide

had a sign that said: YOU MUST BE THIS TALL TO RIDE!

Chillbert was sad, but he tried to be brave

as he watched all his friends zoom away with a wave.

Heading home, he thought, "There's some work I can do!
I'll offer to help on the light-stringing crew!"
He stepped up with Crystal and Drifty and Bob—
but somebody bigger got picked for the job.

When Chillbert got home, he was not feeling good.
He thought, "There's a lot I *would* do if I could!"
His dad said, "You sure could be helpful to me—
let's go to the farm and pick out a nice tree!"

Some Flurryville kids were excited and glad
to hop in the sleigh with their friend and his dad.
They laughed as they left for a time filled with fun—
a colorful crowd in the bright winter sun.

At Perfect Pine farm, they fanned out to explore
some fields and thick woods they had not seen before.
Blizzy discovered a pond that looked nice
and decided to go for a slide on the ice.

CRAAAAACK!!! went the ice. What a terrible break!
The part Blizzy stood on split loose in the lake!
Everyone came when they heard Blizzy shout.
"Help me!" he cried as the ice drifted out.

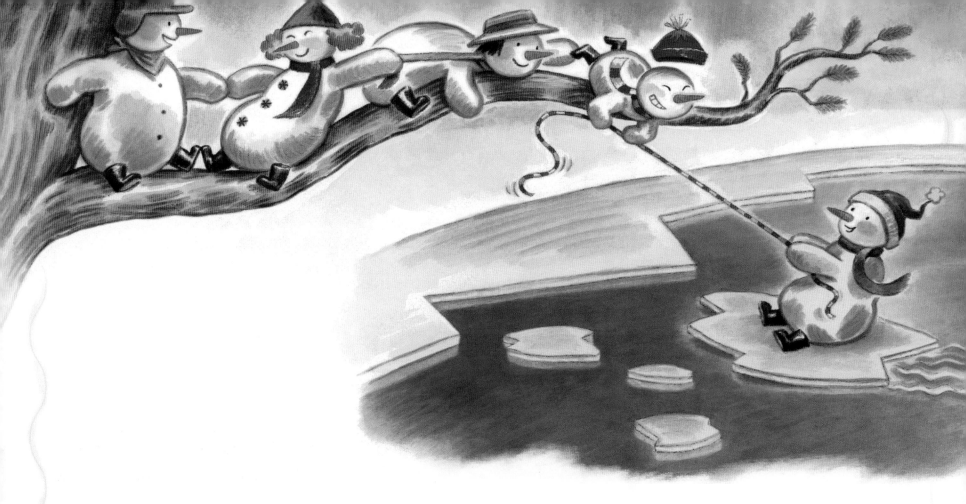

Chillbert spoke up. "Listen! I have a plan!
I'm willing to try it—I think that I can.
I'm short and I'm light; if you hang on to me,
I'll wiggle right out on the branch of that tree!"

So Chillbert climbed up and inched out on the limb,
while his friends joined together and held on to him.
He threw out the rope that he had in his hand
and with one mighty pull tugged their friend to the land.

Everyone cheered, "Chillbert's one gutsy kid!
There's snowbody else who could do what he did!"
His dad was all smiles. "You're the best there could be,
and I'm proud of you, Son. Now, let's pick out our tree!"

Chillbert was thrilled when the chance came along
to show he was kind and courageous and strong.
Even somebody small can be useful and smart,
and you're never too little to have a big heart.

There's Snow Time Like Cookie Time!

A STORY FROM THE HALLMARK HOLIDAY SERIES
Written by Suzanne Heins and Andrew Blackburn
Illustrated by Mike Esberg

Cookies were Snowfred's most favorite food.
And Christmastime always put him in the mood
for a cookie . . . or seven, or maybe a dozen!
(If that's hard to believe, just ask Crystal, his cousin.)

One morning, Snowfred sniffed something so sweet
that it knocked his snow stockings right off his snow feet.
And he knew right away—it just had to be cookies!
After all, Snowfred wasn't a smell-sniffing rookie.

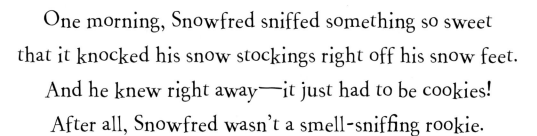

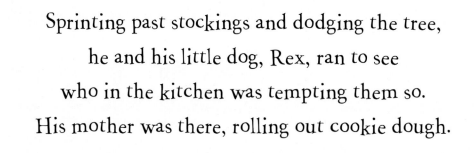

SNIFF
SNIFF

Sprinting past stockings and dodging the tree,
he and his little dog, Rex, ran to see
who in the kitchen was tempting them so.
His mother was there, rolling out cookie dough.

114

"I'm sorry, Snowfred," she said to her son.
"No eating cookies—not even just one!
They're all for the cookie fair later today
when Mittenville's best will be out on display!"

CALLING ALL BAKERS
Mittenville's
12th Annual
Cookie Fair
BRING IT!

Leaving the kitchen, his tummy was rumbly.
Snowdrop, his sister, who saw he was grumbly,
suggested some skating might help him unwind.
But nothing could get cookies off Snowfred's mind.

SKATE RENTAL

"Snowfred," his father said, "come help me, please!
We need some more lights on our house and our trees!"
"How lovely!" Dad said. "See how everything twinkles?"
But Snowfred just saw sparkly cookies with sprinkles!

His brother named Shiverton said with a snort,
"Come on now, Snowfred! Let's build us a fort!"
Afterward, Shiverton said, "Snowfred, lookee!
Why is your side shaped like one giant cookie?"

He sledded. He snowballed. He rode in a sleigh.
And Snowfred survived the whole cookie-less day.

He honestly hadn't believed he could do it.
But evening had come before he even knew it!
It was just about time for the town's cookie fair.
Soon the sweet smell of cookies would be in the air!

Snowfred walked in the door and sniffed such an aroma—
the best smell from Snow York down to old Snowklahoma!
But the kitchen was empty—no cookies were there!
Could they all just have vanished right into thin air?

Then, his mother stepped forward. "I have to admit—
I snuck one and then two. Then I just couldn't quit!"
"I ate some, too," said his dad to his mother.
"Me, three!" said his sister. "Me, four!" said his brother.

"Oh, Snowfred," his mom said. "I asked you to wait.
But the rest of us couldn't! We ate and we ate!
I'm sorry we couldn't stop once we began."
But Snowfred said, "That's OK. I've got a plan."

"I may be the world's number one cookie-eater.
But being with you guys is fifty times sweeter!
So let's make some more! And this time they'll be better.
Because this time we'll make every cookie together."

Magical Sleigh?
SNOW WAY!

A STORY FROM THE HALLMARK HOLIDAY SERIES

Written by Diana Manning   Illustrated by Mike Esberg

Christmas is coming! And here in Chill Valley,
they don't waste a minute—they don't dillydally.
There's the hanging of lights and the holiday shopping,
errands to run and the Christmas-tree chopping!

Sometimes it seems there's so much to be done,
there's hardly time left for the best part . . . the FUN!
But magical things are about to occur,
all thanks to a snowkid named Freezy McBrrr.

Now, Freezy spends time in the family shop—
a quirky garage where ideas never stop.
They take worn-out sleighs and they fix 'em like new
for people to come in and buy when they're through.

Freezy loves helping . . . there's so much to do.
His kid sister Frozemary likes to help, too.
Their dad lets them add their own touch to each sleigh—
though Freezy can sometimes get carried away!

122

One day an old spray can of paint caught his eye—
"Go ahead," said his dad. "Why not give it a try!"
It said "Christmas Spirit" in letters of red,
so he gave it a go, just like his dad said.

When Freezy was finished, that sleigh started rocking—
it rattled and shook in a way that was shocking!
As Freezy jumped into the seat in a hurry,
away went the sleigh in a flash and a flurry!

Nobody knew what was making it go,
but boy, was it fun as it swooshed through the snow . . .
it seemed to go anywhere Freezy desired—
at just the right pace, with no reindeer required!

Word got around about Freezy's new sleigh,
and everyone wanted a ride right away!
The family pitched in as the riders lined up—
Mom served them cocoa in Christmas-y cups.

Grandma and Grandpa stepped in for a ride . . .
they wanted to go for a leisurely glide.
But not Uncle Fridge and Aunt Arctica . . . no!
They wanted that sleigh to just go-go-go-GO!

The snowpeople waited their turn all day long—
that sleigh held some magic that must have been strong.
In line, they all chatted with friends old and new,
while snowkids shared treats and built snowcastles, too!

That night after everyone else had gone home,
Freezy and Dad took a ride of their own,
stopping to look at the beautiful lights—
their favorite tradition on holiday nights.

"Christmas is awesome! And so is this sleigh!"
said Freezy to Dad as they slid on their way.
"But what made it magically go by itself?"
"It was you," Dad replied, "and your choice from the shelf!"

"You know, Christmas Spirit is powerful stuff.
Sometimes just a dab or a spritz is enough.
You helped the whole town take the time for some fun—
you gave them a gift, and I'm proud of you, Son!"

So Freezy helped all of Chill Valley to see
how special the time spent with others can be.
They're never too busy for fun anymore,
'cause they know in their hearts, that's what Christmas is for!

Rex Snows the Way to Grandma's

A STORY FROM THE HALLMARK HOLIDAY SERIES
Written by Diana Manning   Illustrated by Mike Esberg

The Icesnickle family was all loaded up
with goodies and gifts and their lovable pup.
They were headed to Grandma's, for Christmas was near,
and they traveled the long road to see her each year.

But after they'd gone many miles in the snow,
they came to a stop with a "What?" and a "Whoa!"
"There's snow way to get there!" the Icesnickles feared.
No Christmas at Grandma's? Now that would be weird!

Oh, being at Grandma's was always such fun—
she made every Christmas a wonderful one!
She cooked and she knitted, like some grandmas do,
but always took time for a snowball fight, too!

All of a sudden, Rex sniffed at the air—
he knew how to find them another way there.
His keen canine sniffer had picked up a scent,
and off through the snow-covered mountains he went!

SNIFF
SNIFF
SNIFF

His family was puzzled but followed him still
'til they came to a lake by the side of a hill.
Two fun, friendly fellows were fishing away—
that seafood aroma had led Rex astray.

"OK," sighed his family. "I guess we'll keep looking."
And once again, Rex thought he smelled Grandma's cooking . . .

They followed their pup and found Eddie the Yeti
preparing a big batch of Christmas spaghetti!
"You're welcome to join us," said Eddie. "Please stay!"
But the Icesnickles knew they should be on their way.

Rex ran ahead, smelling something divine—
where in the world would they end up THIS time?

They came to a campsite where acorns were roasting
and crashed a big party some squirrels were hosting.

Rex started chasing the squirrels here and there
'til once more he sniffed a new smell in the air.
This time he knew it was Grandma's for sure!
That gingerbread baking just HAD to be her!

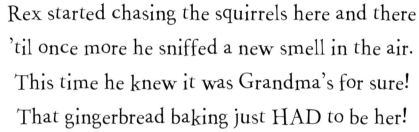

He finally reached Grandma's and barked his "Hello"
then realized his family was back in the snow!

He looked at the mantel and thought of a plan—
he snatched up a stocking and suddenly ran.

He found his whole family back where they had been,
and boy, were they happy to see him again!
"What's this?" wondered Dad, at the yarn he had brought.
"Just what could that pup have been up to?" he thought.

But Rex only barked at the way up ahead,
'til Snow Belle was certain of what he had said.
"He wants us to follow this yarn he's unraveled!"
So off through the snowdrifts to Grandma's they traveled.

The yarn led them right up to Grandma's front door—
she hugged them all tight; then she hugged them some more.
"Good boy!" they told Rex as they patted his head.
"You helped us reach Grandma's by Christmas!" they said.

134

Despite all the detours they had to go through,
just being together was worth it they knew.
Since family, no matter how far or how near,
is what puts the merry in Christmas each year.

And amid all the hugging and munching and talking,
Grandma got busy on Rex's new stocking.
'Cause she knew that Santa was certain to leave
more dog treats than ever on THIS Christmas Eve!

Snow Letter Left Behind

A STORY FROM THE HALLMARK HOLIDAY SERIES
Written by Keely Chace   Illustrated by Mike Esberg

'Twas the very last pickup for holiday mail,
when someone came calling last minute:
"Wait, Mr. Postman! Please open your bag.
This letter just has to go in it!"

The postman was happy to pick up one more,
and he gave his on-time guarantee.
(Sadly, the letter slipped out of his bag,
and nobody happened to see!)

The poor little letter! Left out in the cold!
Would it lie there forever and freeze?
Snow way! In a twinkling, it fluttered and flew
on the *whoosh* of a crisp winter breeze.

It looped through the air, and it landed with care
on a freshly cut tree gliding past.
It kept right on riding until it arrived
by a snow-sprinkled cabin at last.

A welcoming neighbor was waiting outside
with a plate full of cookies—oh, yum!
In all the excitement, the letter filled in
as a napkin to catch cookie crumbs!

The letter was sweeter and sprinklier now,
which attracted a little red friend.
Wheee! The bird snatched it and took to the sky.
Hooray! It was moving again!

The bird flew it swiftly to Snow Central Park,
and she let it drop lazily down.
It fell on a bench seat, its journey all done . . .
unless it could somehow get found!

Well, somebody found the lost letter all right,
when he sat down to snack on a nut.
He rested a spell and then stood up to go
with the letter stuck right to his . . . *pants*.

This gentleman went on his way, unaware,
just a-smiling and tipping his hat.
Finally, a friendly dog snatched it away—
'cause no message should travel like that!

The dog took it quickly and dashed to a spot
where a cool group was jamming along.
The letter picked up on their wintry groove,
riding high on the notes of their song!

From there, it danced on to a magical place
full of all kinds of fun things to try.
It bounced on a seesaw—a snowgirl did, too . . .
and she shot it right into the sky!

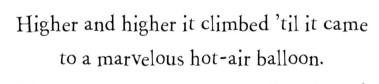

Higher and higher it climbed 'til it came
to a marvelous hot-air balloon.
Here was a great way to travel—yippee!
With some luck, it would reach Santa soon!

Oops! Before long, things began to look wrong.
They'd been heading in quite the wrong way.

141

It seemed like all hope of delivery was doomed . . .
'til they passed by a north-going sleigh!

The boy and his sleigh gladly took it aboard,
and they put on a flying display!
They rocketed north, and at last it appeared
that the letter was well on its way.

Then, at long last, the North Pole came in view
like a peppermint stick up ahead!
The letter swooped downward to make the last push
with some friends zooming by on their sled.

Finally, the letter arrived—right on time—
and old Santa was tickled to get it.
He sensed an adventure between every line,
and he smiled to himself as he read it.

Someone had filled it with joy, he could tell.
Someone had written with care.
Just goes to show, with some magic and love,
Santa's letters will always get there!

If these chilly adventures warmed your heart,
or if perhaps you just liked the art,
we would love to hear from you.

Please write a review at Hallmark.com,
e-mail us at booknotes@hallmark.com,
or send your comments to:

Hallmark Book Feedback
P.O. Box 419034
Mail Drop 100
Kansas City, MO 64141